THE DEVIL CAT SCREAMED

William Morrow and Company   **New York 1966**

THE DEVIL CAT SCREAMED

VERNE T. DAVIS

illustrated by Leslie Goldstein

by the same author

THE TIME OF THE WOLVES

THE GOBBLER CALLED

THE RUNAWAY CATTLE

CONTENTS

1 The Cougar Kills   7

2 Ray Thinks Fast   22

3 Ray Becomes a Cowboy   30

4 Getting Acquainted   40

5 Bear Trouble   50

6 The Cougar Returns   63

7 The Cougar Stalks Ray   74

8 Ray Waits for His Father   89

9 With a Dogsled   104

10 Ray Takes the Trail   113

8.
9.
10.

Chapter 1   THE COUGAR KILLS

"You know, Dad," Ray said to the short, square-built man beside him on the seat of the pickup truck, "I think this British Columbia country must be the prettiest in the world, when all the slopes and valleys start to green up in the spring." Hearing a whine behind them, he glanced back at the hunting dogs in the bed of the screened-in back end of the truck. "It's all right, Spot," he assured one of the four dogs. "We'll soon be there."

Ray turned to look out across the rough, broken

country to the east. The highest peaks were still wearing their heavy caps of snow. "The snow on the mountains looks pretty low for the last of May," he remarked, tucking a mop of red hair back under his cap.

"There was more snow than usual last winter," Mr. McClung said. "Water will be high till late in the season. Not too good for fishing."

The mention of fishing brought something to Mr. McClung's mind. He slapped his coat pocket, then drew out an envelope. "I forgot to mail this letter when we left Trail this morning," he exclaimed. "A fisherman I took out last summer wrote me, asking what was the best time to come up. I told him July. Well, we'll stop at the Kaslo post office."

They pulled up at the small town post office a few minutes later and Ray, not yet fifteen, but sturdily built like his father, slid out of the truck and carried the letter into the office. When he didn't return at once, Mr. McClung touched the horn to hurry him up. This brought Ray to the door. "Mrs. Basker wants you," he called.

"Ray tells me," the postmistress said, when Mr. McClung came in, "that you're going to the Morton ranch. I hear Morton wrote you about the big cougar that has bothered his cattle." Mrs. Basker was looking at them through a window in a wall made up of many little cell-like mailboxes, some of them empty, and some stuffed with letters. "You might pick up another cat a little north of here," she continued. "A cougar killed a yearling up there last night. Stop at the new house just off the road. They'll be glad to see you. You've made yourself quite a reputation, Mr. McClung—you and your dogs," she said, smiling.

When the pickup truck stopped at the new house, the rancher was surprised to see the McClungs and their pack of dogs. "I'm sure glad you're here," he said.

"We heard at the post office that a cougar killed one of your cattle last night," Mr. McClung told him. "Its track should be fresh enough so the dogs can follow it."

The rancher directed them. "Drive up this way about half a mile, then turn to the left on an old logging road. You'll come to what's left of a yearling, right beside the road."

A few minutes later Ray pointed out, "There's the carcass."

Mr. McClung stopped the truck and the dogs began a yelping clamor. They knew what the scent of a fresh kill meant. When Ray turned them loose Old Spot circled wide of the carcass to pick up the outgoing trail. Then he headed off straightaway, the other dogs with him, whining eagerly.

Ray and his father set out at once, each carrying his rifle in one hand so they could move faster. They followed the occasional howls of the pack in the distance as the dogs puzzled out the cold trail. Experience told the hunters the cat wouldn't go far after having eaten such an enormous quantity of meat.

They stopped a moment to listen. Ray's hearing was keen. "They're swinging to the north, Dad," he said, panting. "Shall we cut across in that direction?"

Without wasting breath on speech Mr. McClung nodded, and the two again started the trot that kept them in hearing of the well-trained dogs. Five minutes later Mr. McClung held up his hand. Ahead, the dogs set up a chorus of eager baying which told Ray and his father that the cougar was jumped. "They're barking up, Dad," Ray exclaimed excitedly. "Old Spot is sure making a racket."

Soon they came to the place where the four dogs were milling around a giant fir. When he sighted Ray and Mr. McClung, Old Spot reared up against the trunk of the tree, the high-keyed "barking-up" note of his howls making music to the ears of the hunters.

This was not a new experience for Ray. His father hunted cougars for the bounty paid by the British Columbia government, and Ray had accompanied him several times. These bounty payments plus the value of the skins, trapping in the winter months, and serving as a guide during the fishing and hunting seasons, made Mr. McClung a good living.

Ray started to circle the huge fir, examining every branch and exposed section of the trunk.

His father stood still with his rifle ready, in case the cougar sprang from the tree in an attempt to escape.

When he had reached the side of the tree opposite his father, Ray exclaimed, "I see him, Dad. He's crouched on a big limb close to the trunk."

"Can you see his head?" Mr. McClung asked.

"Part of it. I can see one eye," Ray replied.

"That's plenty," Mr. McClung said. "Bring him down."

Twice before, Ray had been permitted to shoot a treed cougar, but never from so high a tree. He raised his .30-30 caliber carbine. The dogs, sensing the kill, set up a louder clamor, but kept a watchful eye toward the top of the tree. They had seen cougars drop from a great height before.

Ray took his time to sight carefully at the exposed eye. At the crack of his rifle there was a movement among the branches. Then a tawny body swung straight down from the limb, instinctively hanging on a moment with both front paws before plummeting to the ground and landing with a dull *whump*. Mr. McClung's shouted orders did not prevent the excited dogs from closing in, but there was no life in the cat.

"Good shooting, boy," Mr. McClung complimented Ray. "You missed the eye by only an inch."

The dogs soon lost interest in the dead cougar. Old Spot backed away and sat down in a bored manner. He had been through all this many times before.

"Not fully grown," Ray remarked. "About two years old."

"Big enough to collect a bounty," his father said. "Too bad this province isn't paying bounties after the end of this year. And the skin will bring twenty dollars in the States for a rug." He drew his sharp hunting knife and slit the skin down the inside of all four legs and up the middle of the belly. With the skill acquired from much practice, plus some help from Ray, Mr. McClung was rolling up the skin some twenty minutes later.

"Guess we'd better be getting along up the country," he said. "The Mortons will be wondering why we haven't arrived. Lucky, though, we stopped at the Kaslo post office, and found out about this cougar."

When they got back to their pickup truck the dogs, quiet after their run, were put into the screened back end of the truck. They rolled slowly along the highway which paralleled the narrow northern branch of Kootenay Lake. Mr. McClung once stopped the truck to take a look at two elk Ray had spotted feeding in a small open place between brushy hillsides. He stopped again for a minute to watch a brown bear, tearing up a rotten tree trunk in search of grubs. "They know it isn't hunting season," Mr. McClung said, grinning.

Ray smiled back. "We'll soon be there," he remarked, as they left the north end of the lake and continued along the short stretch of river which connected Kootenay Lake with the smaller Duncan Lake. They crossed over the only bridge for many miles up or down the river.

A few minutes later Mr. McClung turned the truck off the road, and drove up a short slope into the yard in front of a ranch house. A spread of corrals and buildings were off to one side. His noisy sounding of the horn brought the Morton family streaming from the house. Ray and his father received a smiling greeting from Mr. Morton, slim and tall, and a more effusive greeting from Mrs. Morton, neither tall nor slim. Three-year-old Susie, with platinum hair and big blue eyes, wasted no time on the visitors.

"Want to see doggies," she cried, running to look into the screen-enclosed bed of the truck,

where the dogs whined and wagged their tails with pleasure at receiving so much attention. Joyce Morton, nine, who had dark hair and hazel eyes in a thoughtful face, followed her little sister to the rear of the truck. She lifted Susie up so she could get a better view of the dogs.

"We expected you earlier," Mrs. Morton told them, "but we waited lunch. Roll out and come in."

As they sat around the table a few minutes later, Mr. McClung remarked, "These Black Angus cattle of yours make fine beef, Morton." He took his second steak from the platter. "Your card said you'd lost another one, to a cougar this time."

"That's right," Mr. Morton replied. "A bear got a yearling a month ago, but they've been out of hibernation for several weeks now, so I don't expect any more trouble from them. Not unless some old grizzly decides that cattle are easier to catch than wild game. This last killing was the work of a big cougar. I might say *the* big cougar, for everyone around here knows about this over-sized cat with two toes missing from his right hind foot."

"Yes, I've heard about him, too," Mr. McClung said, "though I've never been on his trail. How long has he been in this territory? Does he show up in winter? And why hasn't anyone hunted him down before now?"

"Eight years ago," Mr. Morton explained, "a small cougar left his toes in a trap a hunter had set for a wolf. He had chewed off the toes to free him-

self. Since that time this area has been part of his
range. He gets back here every two or three
months, but seldom stays long. We don't always
know in summer when he's around, but his big
tracks show up in winter. He's never been accused
of killing cattle before. Now I hope your dogs will
get on his trail. If they don't find him, he may get
to prefer beef to venison."

Ray was listening with interest. "I'm wondering, too, why he hasn't been hunted down before,"
he said.

"Old Cabbage Kell, the trapper—he was called
that because he always raised plenty of cabbages
in his summer garden patch—took the cougar's
trail several times. The last time was the past
winter. He never came back, but the cougar did."

"Hasn't he ever been hunted with dogs?" Ray
asked thoughtfully.

"Several times," Mr. Morton answered, "but
he always strikes out for the north, to a rough section of country cut up with deep canyons, where
the dogs lose the trail. Seems to be smarter than
most of his kind. Some people think he remem-

bered Old Cabbage Kell's scent around the trap which cost him his two toes. Maybe Kell's pursuit of the cat built up a hate in him for all men."

"Has anybody actually seen him?" Ray asked.

"Yes," Mr. Morton told him. "Vic Rolfe did. He lives up near Trout Lake. Last fall he was cutting wood, and he sat down on a log to eat an apple and rest a bit. The cougar came out of a patch of small pines and started up the hill. A strong wind blowing toward Vic prevented the cat from scenting him. He was getting too close for comfort, so Vic moved his hand to grasp his axe. The cougar stopped to stare at him a moment, unafraid, then turned back into the evergreens as silently as he had come. 'Looked as big as a pony,' Vic said. At least he's bigger than any cougar that has ever been killed in these parts. His tracks in the snow prove that."

"You've talked cougar enough for one time," Mrs. Morton broke in. "You won't be starting a hunt this late in the day, so just loaf around the rest of the afternoon." She turned to Ray and his father. "The Jacksons and the Petties, our nearest

neighbors, are coming over later. This early May
weather is so nice after the long winter, we're
going to the woods to cook up a big feed for
supper. Sort of a picnic. I've got to get busy."

Chapter 2   RAY THINKS FAST

The sun was hanging low when the Mortons and their neighbors and the two McClungs reached a clear spot in the woods where they proposed to spend the fine spring evening. As evidence that this place had been used before, a rough table with long, rustic benches along its sides occupied the center of the spot.

"I guess this old table will stand up for one more time," Mrs. Morton said, leaning her weight on it to test its strength before the baskets of food were set upon one end. "You kids build a fire," she ordered Ray and the several youngsters from the visiting families, ranging from Ray's age down. "You'll have plenty of time to play before dark."

Ray started a small fire from dry pine needles and twigs, while the others scattered out to bring in enough wood to build up the fire and make it last into the evening.

When the flames were leaping high Mrs. Morton, who seemed to take charge naturally of everything going on around her, called, "That's fire enough, boys. Let it burn down so we can cook on the coals."

An old Indian woman had joined the group when they had started for the woods, or, more accurately, had followed at some distance. Now she sat silently on the ground off to one side, but her sharp, black eyes were taking in everything.

Ray caught Joyce alone as she was bringing in a big bunch of wild flowers, which had pushed up here and there through the matted leaves and pine needles of the forest floor. "Where did the old squaw come from?" he asked.

"That's Gurgling Spring," Joyce told him. A

little smile crossed her usually grave features. "That name doesn't fit her very well now, but she says that a long time ago she was the prettiest young squaw in her tribe. She came from some-place far south of here, she says. Her people didn't want her around anymore. They said she was a troublemaker. She claims she talks to the Great Spirit, but that the younger people of her tribe are all educated like white men now, and don't believe in the things the Great Spirit tells her. She's kind of crazy, I guess."

"Where does she stay?" Ray asked, his curiosity aroused. "How long has she been around here?"

"She has a sort of wigwam near the spring above the corrals. She made it from an old tent a city hunter left one fall after hunting season. After it was plain that she intended to stay with us, Pop offered to build her a room, but she said she was born in a tepee and intended to die in one. Mother sees that she has plenty to eat. Pop says she can stay till she dies, so far as he is concerned. She plants a big garden every spring—keeps us in all kinds of vegetables all summer. She catches trout

in the creeks, and snares rabbits in winter." Joyce
stopped to consider. "She's been here three years,"
she finally said. "Yes, that's right. She came when
Mother baked a cake the day I was six. She always
bakes me a birthday cake, with candles and
frosting."

She started to leave him. "I'm going to string
these flowers all down the center of the table,"
she said over her shoulder. "They smell nice."

Ray thought over what Joyce had told him, then
ran to join the rest of the young people in a game
of hide-and-go-seek. There were plenty of hiding
places among the trees and new growth. The par-
ents sat around the table, or tended the cooking at
the fire. Susie played with her white kitten, which
she had insisted on bringing along.

The forest was darkening when Mrs. Morton
called, "Come in, you children. Supper's ready."

Their game was promptly forgotten as they
rushed to the loaded table. Mrs. Morton stayed at
the fire to take care of the big skillets full of steaks
and fried potatoes. Loaves of homemade bread
were on the table, with plenty of butter and plum

jam from last year's crop, along with pickles and two big cakes. There was milk for the younger children, and a bucket of coffee was brewing on three stones bedded in the coals.

Darkness descended before the meal was finished, but most of the group continued to sit around the table, relaxed and enjoying the outing. The smaller children became restive, and left the table to play in the light from the dying fire.

Ray was idly watching Susie as she chased her kitten out to the edge of the flickering firelight. Suddenly he saw something that made him spring to his feet. "Look!" he cried.

The others all looked where he pointed. Not twenty feet beyond the little girl and her kitten, a long, shadowy something was creeping slowly closer to the child. "A cougar," Ray breathed.

Everyone seemed too frozen with surprise and horror to move. Ray thought fast. He knew that no one had brought a rifle to the woods. He sprang away from the table, snatched the bucket of coffee off the coals, and moved quickly toward the slinking form, observing the great size of the animal.

The big cat crouched and bared its long, white teeth as it raised its head, but it made no move to retreat. Not six feet from the snarling cougar, Ray skidded to a stop and dashed the scalding coffee full in the cat's face.

With a frightened scream of pain, the cougar reared back, clawing at its face with its paws. Then it turned and made a wobbling retreat till it disappeared in the dark shadows of the trees.

Ray snatched Susie up and carried her to her mother's arms, the kitten clasped tight to her breast. The group listened in stunned silence as the yowls and screams of pain grew fainter in the distance. Finally they ceased for a moment, then one last, long-drawn-out scream on a different note reached their ears. After that there was silence in the forest.

Old Gurgling Spring had risen to her feet. She came slowly to face Ray. Her blanket fell back upon her shoulders so, for the first time, he could see her dark face. Its leathery skin was criss-crossed by a maze of lines, and wrinkled lips puckered across her toothless gums. But she stood dignified and erect as she said slowly, "He devil cat. He say that only one, either he or you, can live. He hate all men, but hate you most. Unless you kill him, he kill you." Her dark eyes gleamed with conviction.

Drawing her blanket up over her head, she set off through the dark woods toward the ranch.

Chapter 3   RAY BECOMES A COWBOY

The morning after the near tragedy in the woods, Mr. Morton went with Ray and his father to track the cougar. The dogs followed the cold trail straightaway for half an hour, then struck a faster pace. "The trail must be fresher now," Mr. McClung said. "The cougar may have stopped to nurse his scalded face, though I can't imagine anything he might do to relieve the pain."

After following behind the dogs for another two hours, the men caught up with them. They had stopped at the edge of a deep canyon, and showed no inclination to try to make their way down the precipitous sides. Mr. McClung did not urge them.

"When Old Spot says it's time to quit, I believe him," he said. "The cougar isn't apt to come back to this vicinity for a long time, if I know anything about cougars. We can't say for certain till snow comes, but I'd guess your cattle won't be bothered by him this summer, at least, Morton."

They were hungry enough when they returned to the ranch to put away the big midday meal Mrs. Morton had prepared.

"What will you be doing this summer, McClung?" Mr. Morton asked as they loafed around the table, after finishing off the big blueberry pie Mrs. Morton had served for dessert.

"I'll go over to the Vancouver country for a few months," Mr. McClung answered. "Sportsmen come up from the States during the fishing season. I can get plenty of fishermen to take out, as well as others who just want to make trips to enjoy the scenery. I'll be back in this country, though, in the fall when hunting season starts. This is a great section for all kinds of game. Don't know of a better place in Canada."

"What will you be doing, Ray?" Mr. Morton thoughtfully asked. "Will you be going with your father?"

"Yes," Ray answered, looking toward Mr. McClung. "I went with him last summer. Sometimes I can help with the parties he takes out."

"You look strong enough to carry a canoe all by yourself," Mrs. Morton said, smiling across at Ray. "I think I'd feel safe if you were taking care of my party."

Mr. Morton's next words surprised both Ray and his father. "How would you like to stay here and work for me?" he asked. "That is, if your father is agreeable. With a herd of cattle to take care of, and all the other ranch work—haying and harvesting—I'll need some help. I'd pay you a man's wages. I'm sure you're worth it. Mostly you would take care of the cattle. I suppose you've done plenty of riding."

"Since he was able to climb onto a horse," Mr. McClung answered for Ray.

Ray looked at his father. The offer had come as a complete surprise.

"Make your own decision, boy," Mr. McClung said. "Think it over first, though."

No more was said about the matter till after they had left the table. Ray was putting the dogs into the truck for the hundred-mile trip south to the populous city of Trail, where he and his father had lived alone since they had lost his mother four years ago. He was thinking how much he would miss his father, with his yellow-red hair and his honest, freckled Scottish face. They had always been very close, even though they rarely expressed their respect and love for each other.

Ray had been thinking hard about what it would be like to be separated all summer. But he was also thinking how much the money he could earn would help toward the college fund he and his father had started. He would be needing it in another two years. He walked over to the two men, who were standing talking together. "If you're sure it's all right with you, Dad," he said, "I'll stay here with Mr. Morton."

"I think you've made a wise decision, boy," his father told him. "Aside from the money you'll earn, you'll learn something about ranching which may come in handy someday."

But later, watching his father turn south on the highway, Ray couldn't altogether conceal his feeling of loneliness.

Sensing Ray's emotions at finding himself separated from his father at so little notice, and about
to assume a man's responsibility, Mr. Morton said,
"We'll saddle up and take a ride to the upper
pasture, where the herd is feeding."

Ray counted six horses when they entered the
corral. Three of them appeared to be two-year-
olds. A rangy pinto came up to nuzzle in Ray's
pockets in an altogether friendly manner.

"That's Joyce's horse," Mr. Morton said. "He's
hunting for sugar. Joyce has made a pet out of
him. This will be your horse," he continued, slipping a bridle on a stockily built gray. "He's well
trained to work with cattle. I use this bay, but he
isn't broken to handle cattle like this Shorty horse
you'll ride, and Joyce's pinto." He patted the neck
of the handsome dark bay that had come up to him.

Ray was pleased to note how gentle and friendly
all the horses were. They had never been mis-
treated, he concluded.

Arriving at the pasture, Ray was impressed by
the short-legged, heavily built Black Angus cattle.
Scattered out over the slope, the coal-black, horn-

less animals made quite a picture. "How many cattle are in this herd?" he asked.

"Ninety-two right now, with all these calves," Mr. Morton told him. "I don't control pasture for more. These calves replace the three-year-old steers which will be sold in the fall."

Ray started to wonder just what his duties would be. The cattle apparently had been getting along without an attendant. "I've never worked much with cattle," he told Mr. Morton. "What has to be done with them? Do bears and cougars make a lot of trouble?"

"We've had very little loss," Mr. Morton answered. "Cougars seldom bother cattle when deer are plentiful, and if a grizzly starts preying on them the government sends help to hunt it down. The cattle usually can take care of themselves against bears, though some black and brown bears do get big. Lucifer, the bull, guards his herd pretty well. An ordinary bear wouldn't stand much chance against him. I'll show him to you."

They rode on around the herd till they came to an enormous black bull. "Isn't he a beauty?" Mr.

Morton said. "Five years old, and in his prime. He won't grow much bigger."

"I hope he's gentler than he looks," Ray said, looking over the big animal, which was regarding the horsemen with no indication of friendliness.

"He's a bit independent," Mr. Morton answered, "but he's never been mean. He'll soon get used to you, but you might be a little careful around him for a while, especially when you're not mounted. We'll ride around some now, so you can get the lay of the country."

They left the pasture through a barbwire gate, and followed a trail which angled up to higher territory till they came out on a mesa, or bench, of considerable width. Turning their mounts about, they faced down the sloping terrain. Stretching away to the south for many miles was the narrow Kootenay Lake, and they could see, too, small Duncan Lake reaching to the north where it met the Duncan River.

Accustomed to the woods and mountains as long as he could remember, Ray gazed at the scene a long minute in silence. "Pretty country," he said.

Mr. Morton pointed out other benches, small creek bottoms, and trails which Ray would use during the summer. Following Mr. Morton down the trail, Ray soberly considered how little he knew about the work he was going to do, but he had a good feeling that he'd be able to handle the job, and that he would enjoy the summer, too.

Chapter 4 GETTING ACQUAINTED

Mr. Morton had told Ray that the cattle wouldn't be moved out of the fenced pasture for a couple of days, but the next morning he said, "You may as well spend some time getting acquainted with them, Ray. Round up a few from the far corners of the pasture, just to get the feel of it, and to see how well your Shorty horse works. He may be a little rusty, after a winter away from the cattle."

Finding himself alone with the herd in the high pasture, Ray thought over the situation and took account of his equipment and capabilities. Riding the mountain trails with his father on deer and elk hunts had conditioned him for rough country. He would measure up on that score. The rope which was tied onto his saddle was used little as a lasso, Mr. Morton had told him. These animals were not like the half-wild cattle of earlier days, which could be caught and subdued only with the rope. Any branding was done in a chute as the calves passed through. For the most part, the end of the rope served as a persuader to hurry slow or reluctant cattle along. Ray resolved, however, that some of his idle hours with the herd would be spent in practice with the rope.

Mindful of Mr. Morton's suggestion, Ray guided Shorty to a remote section of the pasture where half a dozen cows and their calves were feeding. Riding behind them, he started twirling the end of his rope, and let out a few short yells such as he had heard used by cowboys handling cattle. The cows started slowly in the direction of the main herd, but two of the calves broke away and started back. Shorty veered, quick as a cat, to turn them. Ray almost lost his seat. The little horse cut in behind first one and then the other. He reached over to nip one of them on the hip when it attempted to turn back again. Ray, realizing that he was astride an expert, let the reins hang loose while Shorty, turning this way and that, kept the bunch together as he moved them toward the middle of the pasture.

Noting that Lucifer was observing the maneuver with interest, Ray took pains to ride near him several times as he circulated through the herd. It was just as well to get acquainted with the big bull gradually, he thought.

Since he was not expected back till lunchtime, Ray prepared to spend some time practicing with his rope. A noose was already tied at the end. Nearby was a small stump which made a good target. Time after time, Ray loped Shorty slowly past the stump as he made his cast. He imagined that he could detect a gleam of disgust in the gray horse's eye at each of his failures. For half an hour he worked doggedly with no success. Many times Ray had seen cowboys at ranches and rodeos

dropping their noose over the neck of an animal. The way they did it had looked so easy. Now he realized their skill was the result of years of practice.

But when he finally made a perfect cast, Shorty instantly stopped and braced his feet as though the stump were a living object that would surge against the rope. Ray's respect for Shorty increased as the horse displayed the perfection of his training.

He left off his practicing and was about to start down to the ranch when a bright beam of light played about him, once crossing his eyes with a blinding glare. Joyce was flashing a mirror, as she had told him she would when it was time to come in for lunch.

Mr. Morton was amused at Ray's enthusiasm as he told all about how he had spent the morning. "You'll get a real workout tomorrow," he said, "when we move the herd. We're taking them down to one of the creek bottoms where there's plenty of feed. The higher benches will be good later."

Ray spent the rest of the day helping Mr. Morton reshingle one of the farm buildings—new work
for him. He found it was fun, because like all
boys he liked to drive nails. He looked over the
even rows of shingles with satisfaction when they
finished. He felt sure he would enjoy living with
the Mortons.

Ray began to get a better understanding of
what handling a big herd of cattle meant when,
the next day, the cattle were turned out of the
pasture. Mr. Morton rode his dark bay horse,
Mahogany, saying, "He needs training. I may as
well break him in."

"I want to go, too," Joyce said. "I can help."

"I guess you might at that," her father said
thoughtfully. "You and your pinto horse can be
very useful, but don't do any reckless riding."

It was not a long move, but the cattle insisted
upon stopping to graze on the lush new grass
along the way, and had to be constantly rounded
up from the rear and sides to keep them together
and moving in the right direction. Joyce on her
pinto was perfectly at home in this business. The

horse could stop short and spin around to head off a stubborn steer quite as smoothly as Ray's Shorty.

Well before noon, the herd reached the new grazing grounds. They would be kept there till feed became so short that a move to new feeding grounds was necessary. After staying about an hour to get the cattle settled down, Mr. Morton

and Joyce left Ray to spend the rest of the day with them. "So long as the feed is good, the cattle will graze along this creek," Mr. Morton said. "Let them work up the creek. The valley widens out above here, then it pinches down to a canyon. They can't get out that way."

After midday most of the cattle, well filled with the new grass, lay down to rest and peacefully

chew their cud. Ray took the opportunity to explore his surroundings. Sweaty from the unaccustomed work, he took a dip in a deep hole in the little stream. The water was icy cold, but he felt fine after he had used his shirt for a towel to partially dry himself. Wandering along the bank, he observed trout darting across the shallows. An ardent fisherman, Ray always carried some trout flies in his suitcase. Now he resolved that he would stick a few in his hat.

He rode a mile up the valley and found that it indeed widened out. The herd should find good grazing for a week before it would be necessary to take them to new pasture. When they did move, the growth where they now were feeding would freshen up and make good grazing again later.

While the sun dropped below the mountains to the west, Ray circled the herd to collect them into a closer group, as he had been told to do. The cattle would not separate too widely, and he would be back in the morning to round them up again. According to Mr. Morton, that would be the procedure all summer.

Thinking over his day's work as he headed for
the ranch, Ray had a fine feeling of satisfaction.
Work could be enjoyable and entertaining if one
were honest in his efforts to do a good job. Riding
along, he sang what he remembered of the range
songs he had heard the cowboys up from Montana
sing at the rodeos. Shorty pricked up his ears as
though he had heard them before.

Chapter 5 BEAR TROUBLE

After spending two months with the Morton herd, Ray had learned much that made his work easier. Some of the excitement he had felt during the first weeks on the benches and bottoms of the range had worn off, but he still thoroughly enjoyed the days spent alone with his herd. The cattle had become accustomed to him, and by frequently bringing a carrot or turnip from Gurgling Spring's garden, he had made friends with the big bull, Lucifer.

"You take what you want from garden," the old

Indian woman had told him. "You be careful of devil cat," she added. She seldom failed to mention the cougar when she was speaking with him. "Some day he come back," she would say darkly. "He not forget."

Ray always listened respectfully to her prophecies of evil, but took little account of the words of warning. "It's no wonder her people didn't want her around any longer," he told Mrs. Morton, after one of these conversations. "Does she always prophesy death and disaster?"

"Not always," Mrs. Morton told him. "Last summer a little girl wandered away from a party on a fishing expedition. They felt certain she had gone down to the rocky shore of a lake in the vicinity, and had fallen in. But the old woman told them, 'No, not drown; she go up creek long ways. You hurry. Bad hurt.' "

"Did they find the little girl?" Ray asked.

"Yes," Mrs. Morton answered. "Old Charlie Hopp, who guides fishing parties in summer, and uses a dog team after the snow gets deep, went up the creek with two neighboring ranchers. Hopp took his lead dog along, and the dog found the little girl. She had walked a long way, and then fallen over a cliff. She was badly hurt, but she came out of it all right. You wouldn't be able to convince those people, or Charlie Hopp either, that Gurgling Spring doesn't see things we can't."

Mrs. Morton's round face became thoughtful for a moment. "She has told me about other things which came true, and some of the things couldn't be credited altogether to the insight of a woman who has lived a long life under circumstances most of us know little about. But don't look so serious." She broke off, smiling. "I don't want you to think I'm a witch, too."

Sometimes, when the cattle were being pastured close to home, Joyce rode out on her pinto. "I'm teaching him a trick," she said one day. "I want him to come when I blow this whistle, no matter where he is. And you can help me, Ray."

"What shall I do?" Ray asked.

"Ride Pinto over past that bunch of trees," Joyce directed him, "and turn him loose. He won't wander far if you throw the reins over his head.

He's been trained that way, just like Shorty. If he comes when I whistle, I give him a lump of sugar."

Ray rode the pinto beyond the trees and dismounted, tossing the reins over the horse's head. He watched Pinto, a little taller and rangier than Shorty, as he grazed around the spot, careful not to step through the reins. When the sound of Joyce's whistle reached his ears, the pony threw up his head to listen, but didn't make a move till the whistle sounded a second time. Then, holding his head high so his feet wouldn't become entangled in the reins, he galloped away to his mistress to get a lump of sugar.

Joyce was not satisfied till, after several trials on other days, Pinto would come to Ray, too, when he was the one to blow the whistle.

"He's smart," Ray remarked, after the horse had thoroughly learned the trick.

"He's fast, too," Joyce said, pridefully stroking the pinto's neck. "A man who races horses wanted to buy him last summer. Pop wouldn't think of selling him. He's plenty quick on the getaway,

too. Come on, I'll show you. We'll line both horses up, and I'll race you to the trees."

Supporting the reputation his mistress had given him, Pinto left Shorty a length behind in the first three jumps, though Shorty did well enough after he got going.

"You see," Joyce said proudly, "he's quick on the start, like a racehorse. He can run faster than he just did, too."

Watching the pinto carry her away down the

mountain at a cautious canter, Ray wondered what would have taken the place of horses for Joyce if she had been raised in a big city. Here they were the greatest thing in her life. "She'll have those two-year-olds broken for bareback riding before I ever get around to cinching a saddle on them," Mr. Morton had said.

Ray could easily understand how one could love this beautiful, half-wild mountain country. He was never lonesome out on the range with the big black cattle, fat and sleek in their summer coats. And a day seldom passed that he did not see some of the game animals which were so plentiful. Deer came to the streams for water, showing little fear of Ray so long as he made no threatening move. Any morning he was apt to find elk cows and their calves feeding with the herd, and one time a big bull elk, shedding the velvet from its high, six-point horns, was with them. Moose were more suspicious of the boy and his horse, but he sometimes caught glimpses of them as they left some marshy shore when they scented his approach.

But everything had been running too smoothly

to last. One morning in late July, Ray rode out to
find that his cattle were not grazing on the high
mesa where he had left them the night before.
This mesa was the highest pasture used during the
summer. On two sides the edges fell away almost
vertically to the valley below, and the mountain
wall rose steeply at the rear. A flowing spring at
the base of the mountain furnished water for the
herd. On the fourth side, the land sloped steeply
away into something like a trail. There the tracks
indicated that the cattle had left on the run.

Ray found the herd a mile below. They were
spread out over a partially wooded slope. He
rounded them up and drove them down to a small
creek bottom, then rode back to the high ground
where he had left them the night before. Circling
the area, he found the cause of the cattle's flight.
Behind a clump of bushes at the foot of the mountain was what remained of a yearling. Shorty
snorted at some scent which disturbed him.

Ray dismounted and looked for tracks. He
found enough in a soft spot to prove that a bear
had killed the yearling—a big bear, though he

didn't believe the tracks were large enough to have been made by a grizzly. He rode to the ranch to tell Mr. Morton what had occurred.

"This is mighty disturbing," Mr. Morton said. He paced back and forth a minute, thinking it over. "It's been two years since we've had cattle killed in the summertime. Once bears start preying on cattle, they're apt to continue, and the only remedy is to hunt them down. They rarely get so bold as to come out in daylight, though. Well, we'll move the herd clear out of that territory. The rains have kept the feed good a couple of miles south of here."

When two weeks passed with no sign of the bear, the move seemed to have been a good one. Grazing was excellent. "I can almost see the young stock growing," Ray told Mr. Morton. There was good fishing in the creeks, too, and Ray brought in strings of fine trout for the Morton table, and for old Gurgling Spring, whom he always remembered.

One day Ray was turning back a few of the young stock from the lower end of a creek bottom, which spread out above the banks of the stream to make a high meadow. Suddenly he heard a commotion farther up the meadow. Looking up, he saw a monstrous black bear. Apparently it had rushed out of the concealing thicket to strike down a calf, for it was starting back to the brush, half carrying, half dragging its kill.

A swift regret that he had not kept a rifle with him crossed Ray's mind; he had figured it would be too much in the way when he rode through the brush. Now he urged Shorty to a gallop and made his way through the cattle, which were running from the bear. Riding straight toward the animal, he scarcely knew just what he could do if it refused to retreat. The bear seemed to have all the best of the situation.

Then he saw that one member of the herd was not running away. Lucifer was going to the rescue. He was charging directly at the killer.

The bear dropped the calf and reared up to defend itself against this attacking fury, as Lucifer, with lowered head, came pounding toward it. He knocked the bear onto its back, but the big animal struck with a paw at Lucifer's head and broke the force of the bull's charge. Before the raging Lucifer could follow up his advantage the bear, with surprising agility, was on its feet.

Shorty came to a stop at what he considered a safe distance from the fighting pair, but the bear paid no attention to Ray's shouts. Desperate for some means of stopping the savage conflict, which might end any minute in death or serious injury to the valuable bull, Ray seized the rope coiled over the horn of his saddle. Slipping the knot to make a wide noose, he swung the rope and shouted with all his lungs. The bear gave him an angry glance, but continued to concentrate on fending off Lucifer's butting head.

Ray's judgment told him he might be in mortal danger if he found himself and a full-grown bear on opposite ends of a thirty-foot rope. But the bear was attempting to clamp its jaws on the neck of the fast-moving but hornless bull. When Ray saw blood spurt from a gash made by the bear's slashing jaws, he hesitated no longer. He urged Shorty to move closer to the fighting animals. He was swinging the rope as he had during his several weeks of practice. He prayed that his cast might be good. Noticing Ray's approach, the bear reared a little higher and raised its head. Then the hours of practice paid off. The noose settled neatly about the big animal's neck.

Shorty turned back in fright, completely upsetting the bear. The cow pony braced his feet to keep the rope taut. Unable to defend itself, the bear became a victim of the choking rope and the crushing plunges of the bull, which again and again threw the full force of his 1600 pounds down upon the ribs of the fallen bear, till it became motionless.

Ray loosened the hitch from the pommel of the saddle and eased away. He felt much safer with a greater distance between himself and the wrought-up bull until Lucifer's temper had cooled.

Rounding up the cattle, Ray stayed with them half an hour to quiet them down, then set out for the ranch to tell Mr. Morton what had taken place.

When Mr. Morton returned with Ray an hour later, Lucifer had joined the herd. He was tired

and docile, and permitted his master to sponge his wounds with disinfectant. "Some of these wounds are deep," Mr. Morton said, "but they'll probably heal quickly. He's strong and healthy, and the blood washed out the cuts pretty well."

He looked Ray over with approval. "In dropping a noose over the head of a six-hundred-pound bear, you sure were inviting trouble," he said. "I'll say it took plenty of nerve. This bull comes from the finest breeding stock in this province. His pedigree runs back two hundred years. You have saved me the equivalent of your summer's wages today."

Chapter 6 THE COUGAR RETURNS

After he and Lucifer together had killed the bear, Ray made a point of keeping his rifle in a scabbard tied to his saddle. He considered it unlikely that he would ever see another bear, but he was taking no chances.

A week after the event, the old Indian woman was waiting at the corral when Ray went to saddle Shorty. Wisps of gray hair framed her wrinkled face. She looked him over reflectively. "Hear devil cat cry up on mountain last night," she said. "Say

face hurt and him come back to kill you. You
better watch. Him cunning devil."

"I'll be careful," Ray assured her. She shook her
head and turned away, muttering something in
her native tongue.

As he rode off, Ray thought over the warning
Gurgling Spring had given him. She may have
heard a cougar scream up on the mountain, he
concluded, but it could have been any cougar. He
didn't credit her with recognizing the scream of
any one particular animal. Being alone so much
and brooding over her past troubles had no doubt
affected her mind—had made her a little crazy and
notional in regard to certain things she heard or
saw. Besides, he had heard arguments between
old-timers about whether cougars did or did not
scream. Some claimed they made a sound like a
baby's cry. However, he had certainly heard the
big cat give out screams of pain when he had
doused it with scalding coffee. And he could recall
vividly the great size and the snarling lips of the
crouched cougar before the coffee struck it. He
would take the old woman's warning seriously,

he resolved. His rifle would never be far from his hand.

Shorty stepped briskly along, for the morning air was crisp. Ray was thinking that he had done well in having his school books sent to the ranch, so he could keep up with his class until the cattle had been brought in off the range for the winter. Mr. Morton had asked him to stay till that time. "By the first of October, we usually have snow on the higher pastures; sometimes earlier," he had said.

Leaving the trail to take a shortcut to the cattle, Ray guided Shorty over the rougher terrain. When Shorty gathered himself to leap across a shallow depression, Ray naturally leaned forward in the saddle. But the usually surefooted animal slipped and fell short. His knees struck the opposite side of the dry run, and Ray went flying over his head.

Coming up unhurt, Ray looked his horse over, as any good horseman would. Shorty had a deep gash in one knee where a sharp edge of rock had cut it. When Ray led him around, he limped badly. Ray patted the pony's neck. "I'd better get you back home before this knee stiffens up," he told Shorty.

Throwing down his leather jacket, he stripped off his shirt and used it to bandage up the injured knee, which was bleeding badly. Then, picking the way carefully, he led Shorty back to the trail and down to the ranch.

"This leaves us one horse short," Mr. Morton

said, after examining the cut. "I'll sew this up, but it'll be several weeks before Shorty can be used." He considered a moment. "I guess you'll have to ride Pinto," he said. "He's the only well-trained horse we have left."

Pinto soon proved his worth as an all-around cow pony. He was younger and quicker than Shorty, so the switch in horses did not inconvenience Ray at all. Also, he could be trusted to stay in the vicinity of any spot where he might be left, carefully keeping his feet from becoming entangled in the trailing reins as he cropped the grass. Ray tried Pinto out several times with the whistle Joyce had given him when he started riding the little horse. Pinto always came galloping at the second blast of the whistle and nuzzled in Ray's pocket for the sugar he expected.

One morning when Ray reached the place where he had left the herd, he again found them scattered. This time he scouted the territory before rounding up the cattle, and he found the carcass of a two-year-old steer. Carefully going over the ground, Ray discovered several huge cougar tracks, some of which showed that two toes were missing from one of the cat's hind feet. Old Gurgling Spring's warning had not been all idle talk. The big cougar had come back. Ray slid his rifle from the scabbard tied to Pinto's saddle, though he knew there was little likelihood of the cougar being near after the big meal it had made off the steer.

The cougar had eaten away a shoulder to get into the soft inner meat—the heart and the liver. There was evidence that it had shaved most of the hair off the skin with its sharp teeth before it had torn into the flesh. Ray could imagine the cougar's slow, patient stalk behind the bushes till it had approached close enough to make a quick rush and spring to the back of the unsuspecting steer. Then the clamp of its long fangs deep into the neck of the luckless animal. No doubt a powerful forepaw had reached out to give the head a twist which would snap the spine. Ray lifted the head by an ear. Yes, the neck was broken.

Though his judgment told him that the big cat

had put a wide distance between itself and its kill before lying up to sleep and digest its big meal, Ray rounded up the cattle with his rifle in his hands.

He was thinking over the letter he had received the day before from his father. "I can't leave this Victoria country till the first week in October," Mr. McClung had written. "I've been pretty busy all summer, and now I've agreed to take out several hunting parties. I'll be up there just as soon as I get back home."

That meant Ray could expect his father about the time Mr. Morton had said they'd take the cattle in for the winter. Ray would be glad to see him again, and to go home, too, though he had enjoyed the summer in the mountains and he knew that Mr. Morton was pleased with the way he had taken care of the cattle.

After getting the herd bunched, Ray rode in for a conference with Mr. Morton. The rancher looked discouraged when Ray told him about finding the dead steer. "It's too bad we couldn't have got through the rest of the season without this happening," he said. "Another three weeks, and they'll be brought in; at least, they'll be run only in the bottoms right around home. The hay for winter feeding won't hold out if we bring them in now." Mr. Morton paused a moment to consider the problem. "Well, the cougar isn't apt to strike again for a few days. We'll leave them out and see what happens. Better not move them back onto that bench, though. We'll let the steer's carcass lie where it is to see if the cougar comes back to feed off it."

Ray moved the cattle as directed, but rode back every day to see whether the cougar had returned to its kill. It returned the second night to fill up on the still fresh meat, and again two nights later. It came no more after that.

Ray took to scouting every day in the vicinity of the cattle's feeding grounds. When a week had gone by since the cougar had killed the steer, he began to hope that it had returned to its previous habit of living off deer and other animals. But one morning Ray found a few fresh tracks not far from the place he had left the herd the night before.

The cougar had approached near enough to observe the cattle, but apparently they had not got scent of it.

Ray sat on his horse and concentrated upon this development for some time. There was no doubt in his mind that the cougar was staying in the vicinity, intent upon making another kill. Some measures must be taken to protect the herd; but what? There was little probability that it would attack during the daylight hours, but after dark the cougar might become more daring. Ray certainly did not intend to permit this overbold predator to scare him off the range. Still, he hoped it was only the cattle that interested it.

Finally an idea took shape in Ray's mind. Joyce had a small tepee tent set up in the backyard for a playhouse. It was only about six feet square, and made of the usual brown, waterproofed canvas. If he brought it out and set it up near the bedding grounds of the herd every night, this strange contraption would make the cougar suspicious. With the flaps securely tied, Ray felt that he would be quite safe, even if the big cat were inclined to make him trouble.

Taking the trail that led toward the ranch, Ray swung the pinto into a lope which would soon cover the two miles to the Morton ranch.

Chapter 7 — THE COUGAR STALKS RAY

Arriving at the ranch, Ray found Mr. Morton doing fall plowing some distance from the house. He was pleased to find him alone, because it gave them a chance to talk over in private the danger to the cattle, and to discuss his plan for protecting them at night. He didn't want to alarm Mrs. Morton.

Mr. Morton listened to Ray explain that when the cougar's keen scent told it that the small canvas house was occupied by a man, it would be too suspicious to come close to the herd.

"You may be right about that, but you'd be taking a chance, Ray. I would never forgive myself if something happened to you. The cattle aren't worth it."

However, finally persuaded by Ray's argument, Mr. Morton unhooked his team and headed for the barn. He said to Ray, riding along beside him, "I really should inform the authorities in Victoria that we have a cattle-killing cougar here; they'd send someone with dogs to hunt it down."

"Dad will be here soon," Ray told him. "I wrote him to be sure and bring the dogs. There's no better pack in the province, and no better hunter than Dad. I'm sure I won't be in danger, because I won't be wandering around after dark, and I'll keep a good fire going till the cattle are all bedded down and I'm ready for bed."

Joyce was still at school when they took down her play tent, but Mrs. Morton was curious about why Ray should suddenly decide to stay with the cattle at night as well as all day. "Has that cougar been bothering the cattle again?" she asked suspiciously.

"We just don't want him to kill another critter," Ray told her. "I'm going to stay out with them the rest of the season, if you'll fix me up with some food. I can ride in anytime during the day when I get low on supplies."

"You should have a packhorse," Mrs. Morton said, laughing, when Ray prepared to ride away. The tightly rolled little tent was tied, with a pack of food, behind the cantle of the saddle. Some cooking utensils hung on the horn, and a picket pin for staking out Pinto was tied on the side.

Old Gurgling Spring stepped out from behind a shed as he rode by. No doubt she had guessed the meaning of all the activity when she saw Ray taking down the tent. She raised her hand to stop him, but she had no words of warning this time. She just shook her head and handed him a small buckskin pouch. "Maybe help," she said, her eyes glowing somberly. "You keep all the time." She turned back, still shaking her head sorrowfully as Ray rode away.

Opening the little pouch, Ray took out a piece of buckskin the size of a silver dollar, beaded with

a curious design. He put it in his pocket. He would do as she had told him about keeping it with him, though he did not believe in charms.

Back with his cattle, Ray used his hand ax to cut three poles to hold up the peak of the tent. Then he set it up. While he was getting a supply of firewood, Lucifer came over slowly to smell the tent. He turned away, apparently satisfied that it was nothing to worry about. The bull had become more friendly since the episode of the bear, as if he realized that it had been teamwork by the two of them that had disposed of the bear, rather than just his own attack.

Darkness was not far away when Ray rounded up the herd, crowding them near the tent. They were well stuffed with the rank growth on the meadow and would soon settle down for the night. The pinto he staked out close to one side of the tent.

By the time these preparations for the night were finished the sun had dropped behind the mountains in the west. A feeling of loneliness came over Ray as the long shadows were blotted out by descending dark. Ray had spent many nights in the woods with his father, but he had never spent one entirely alone. Added to his loneliness was an uncomfortable sensation that he was being watched from someplace beyond the firelight. However, plain reason told him that so long as the stock were quiet, nothing could be lurking too close.

He set about steeping tea, which he had found in the pack Mrs. Morton had made up for him. Sandwiches and tea made a good supper. He was tired, for he had spent a busy day. Becoming sleepy, he spread his blankets on the canvas floor of the little tent, with his rifle laid close beside them. The fire had died down to a bed of coals when, after taking a last look at the cattle and his horse, he went inside and tied the flaps with bow-knots, which he could quickly jerk loose.

Stretched out in his bed, Ray thought about the strange situation he found himself in, but his eyes insisted upon closing. He hoped, as he dropped off to sleep, that any stirring of the cattle would wake him.

Ray didn't wake up till the morning light struck the tent. Finding everything quiet outside and the cattle scattering out to feed, Ray ate breakfast, saddled his horse, and rode around the far edges of the meadow, checking any soft or sandy spots for possible tracks. He found nothing to indicate that the cougar had been prowling in the vicinity.

Ray followed this procedure for the next few days. Nothing disturbed the cattle either during the day or night, and he was beginning to think that the cougar was too suspicious of the tent and constant presence of the herdsman to make more trouble. But that night he was awakened by the cattle's stirring and snorts of alarm from Pinto. He jerked open the flaps and stepped outside, rifle in hand.

By the dim light of a half-moon, Ray could see the cattle all facing the nearest approach to the wooded fringe surrounding the bed-grounds. Pinto had retreated to the end of his rope and was looking off toward the timbered slope, too, from which a strange sound came. It began on a low key, reminding Ray of a crying baby. Then it rose in volume and ended in a sort of scream. The eerie sound caused a prickling sensation to creep up Ray's spine. There was no doubt that it was the cry of a cougar.

He raised his rifle and sent two bullets crashing toward the woods. The sound ceased abruptly. Then Ray built up his fire and sat by it till daybreak, with his rifle across his knees. He knew that he would receive ample warning from Pinto and the cattle if the prowler came close. But nothing out of the ordinary was heard for the remainder of the night.

For the next several nights there was no disturbance. One evening the cattle drifted farther from the tent than usual before they lay down for the night, but Ray did not think it was worth the bother to bring them back. Late that night the pounding of hooves woke him from a sound sleep, and he started up in bed, his rifle coming instinctively into his hands. There was a snuffling sound outside, followed by the soft sound of digging under the opposite side of the tent. Pointing the rifle toward the noise, Ray shot twice. He heard something spring back from the tent and go bounding away.

Ray could feel cold sweat breaking out on his forehead, but he resolutely forced himself to open the flaps. Pinto, tied to the picket pin, would be vulnerable to attack. But when he stepped outside into the moonlight to look for the horse, he was gone. In his fright, Pinto had pulled the pin and left with the cattle.

Ray didn't believe that the cougar would come again that night; at any rate, he had no intention of rounding up the cattle in semidarkness. He stoked the fire, and blew his whistle for Pinto, though he had little conviction that the frightened pony would heed its call. But the well-trained little horse soon showed up, dragging the rope and the picket pin. With his ears pricked forward, he stopped every few steps to scent the air before advancing a few feet nearer to Ray and the fire. Ray untied the rope from the horse's halter. He was sure that Pinto would stay close to him till morning. He could trust the horse to warn of danger, too.

Ray had ample time now to think over the cougar's actions. He concluded it was far less interested in the cattle than it was in their herdsman. Never before had he heard of a cougar hunting a man, but there could be no doubt about the intentions of the animal which had started to dig under his tent. He was thankful for the canvas floor that was sewed to the sides of the tent. Ray took from his pocket the little pouch the old Indian woman had given him and looked at it a long time. He wondered if the charm had helped protect him in any way. He was beginning to believe that Gurgling Spring really could foretell things of the future—at least, he now believed her statement that the cougar was out to get him.

The next morning, when he told Mr. Morton the occurrence of the night before, the tall man thought for a long time. "Perhaps we'd better bring in the cattle, Ray," he said. "I don't think you're safe out there alone. I'll saddle up and help you bring them in. I'm not thinking of the loss of another head of stock. If this cougar should attack the herd at the end opposite your tent, the cattle might stampede right over the tent. Of course, it will mean a longer feeding period if they're brought in now; I'll have to buy more hay."

But Ray had another idea. "This cat never shows up during the day," he said. "I'll take a lantern with me, and hang it to a tent pole above the tent. I'm sure that will keep him away."

Mr. Morton reluctantly agreed. "The snows may start by the first of October. There's only one week of September left," he said.

So Ray returned alone to the herd. He replaced one of the poles of the tepee tent with a long one which extended well above the peak. Before retiring for the night, he lifted the lantern on a forked stick to hang it upon the tent pole. He felt certain that the cougar would consider it some kind of menace, and would keep its distance. This proved true. Three nights passed without incident, and Ray found no tracks on his daily scouts about the territory, with his rifle in his hand, resting upon the pommel of his saddle. He began to feel quite safe, especially in daylight.

Three days after the cougar's sneak attempt to dig under the tent, Ray decided to catch a few trout for supper. He dismounted and cut a pole. The trout were not biting as well as usual, and he had left the herd and Pinto some distance up the creek before he had pulled in the number he wanted.

As he was winding up his line, Ray turned and

caught a glimpse of the long tail and hindquarters of a cougar slinking behind a big boulder near the edge of the creek. He had no doubt that his enemy was stalking him. Ray thought fast. He was between the cougar and the cattle, but he was certain that if he started to run the big cougar would give chase, as a cat would chase a running mouse. He would be pulled down before he got well started.

Then an idea struck him. He took the whistle from his pocket and blew a sharp blast. In a moment he blew again, being careful not to move, because he was certain the cougar was watching him through the screen of bushes surrounding the big boulder. He hoped the shrill whistle might confuse the cougar as well as summon Pinto.

In a moment he heard the beat of Pinto's hooves. Soon he came in sight, trotting down the path with his head carried high and to one side as usual, to keep his feet clear of the reins. He came mincing up to Ray, expecting the usual lump of sugar. Catching the reins in one hand, Ray seized

the pommel with both hands just as the horse caught sight of the cougar easing out from behind the boulder. The little horse spun on his heels as Ray sprang into the saddle. The quick start and speed that Joyce had claimed for him were all that saved Ray and the horse from the dash of the cougar. It was only a few feet behind the horse's heels when Pinto really got into his stride. He galloped up a sloping path to the top of the high bank. As he sped across the clear space of meadow, Ray glanced back. The cougar had stopped at the edge of the screening bushes.

Sliding his rifle from the scabbard, Ray rode back to the point where the cougar had disappeared. He patrolled the high bank for some distance up and down, feeling safe so long as he had the rifle in his hands, but he saw nothing of the animal. Ray felt certain that the cougar wouldn't disturb the cattle during the remaining hours of daylight. He decided to ride in to the ranch and report the skulking attack.

Ray was shaken by the experience he had just come through. It had been close—too close! A horse less quick would never have escaped the claws of the cougar. He patted the pinto's neck in appreciation as they moved along.

Some time later, after having been told what had taken place, Mr. Morton looked at the sinking sun. "There isn't time to bring the herd in today," he said. "I'll ride out and stay with you tonight. We'll bring them in tomorrow."

Chapter 8   RAY WAITS FOR HIS FATHER

Ray was not idle during the week he spent waiting for his father to come to the ranch. Light snow had appeared on the higher levels, and all the peaks were heavily covered. But since the area around the ranch was still bare, the cattle were turned out to feed every day, and were brought back to the ranch every night. Now that the herd was so near to home, Mr. Morton didn't consider it necessary for anyone to stay with them.

"You might try for a deer," he told Ray one morning. "The weather is cool enough so meat will keep now. I often hang up a couple while they're in good condition, but I have things to do. You bring in the venison. You may run across an elk, too, though they usually hang high till the snow gets deeper."

So, after pushing the herd out to pasture, Ray rode Pinto across a low divide and down into another creek bottom. Finding plenty of signs of deer there, he tied the horse and hunted on foot. He stayed well up from the creek, so he could see across to the opposite side of the little valley, knowing that deer had a habit of spending the day near the upper end of a draw. If jumped by a hunter they would go up and over the hill, and soon be out of sight.

His knowledge served Ray well. When he neared the point where the small stream died out against the rising slope, a band of two does and several small deer broke from cover and ran up over the hill. But Ray held his fire, for he knew a buck might be hiding in the cover. A buck usu-ally stayed quiet till the hunter's attention was fixed upon the does, then it stole out in another direction, if it could remain screened from sight. If not, it would make a quick dash away.

A full minute passed before Ray saw movement on the brushy opposite slope of the draw. He caught glimpses of horns as the buck moved higher up the slope. Forced to come out into the open, where the growth died out, it began to run. Ray started shooting. He missed the moving target twice, but his third shot dropped the buck.

He dressed out the deer, and went to bring up Pinto. The horse had packed deer before, and stood quietly while Ray struggled to load the buck, which was bigger than himself, across the saddle. It took all his strength, but he finally succeeded, and led the horse home.

Later in the week Ray went above the ranch to do some scouting in the light snow that covered the benches. He was looking for cougar tracks, but found none. He did run into a band of elk, however, and shot a young bull that would make good eating.

This time he had to bring Mr. Morton up to help pack the meat down to the ranch. "With the deer you brought in," Mr. Morton said, looking over the elk loaded on the horses, "we have plenty of meat for the time being."

Arriving back at the ranch, they found that Mr. McClung had come in. Ray was so glad to see his father that he could have hugged him, but his Scottish conservatism made him self-conscious. After shaking his hand, Mr. McClung looked his son over, and clapped him on the back.

"You look tough and healthy, boy," he said. "You must be two inches wider, and about that much taller. Work has agreed with you."

"Yes, and it's mighty interesting, too," Ray said. "Now I'm going to let the dogs loose before they scratch a hole in the screen."

The dogs all romped around Ray, but it was to Old Spot that he gave most of his attention. Ray squeezed him as the old dog reared up onto him. After all, Spot had been with them eight years. He was wise in the ways of cougars. The pack followed his lead.

His father looked grave when Ray told him about his experience with the cougar. "I didn't want you to worry," Ray said, "so I didn't write about it."

"I've never heard of a cougar really stalking a man," Mr. McClung said thoughtfully. "They'll fight if they're cornered, but they'd rather run, or climb a tree. When he crept up on little Susie was another time this cougar showed less fear of men than they usually do. We must destroy him before he does kill someone." Mr. McClung paused a moment. "Those clouds hanging over the mountains promise snow tonight. We'll make a swing tomorrow out over the territory where you herded the cattle, Ray, to look for fresh tracks in the snow. We'll leave the dogs here until we find out whether he's still hanging around."

Mr. McClung's prediction about snow falling proved to be well founded. The hunters made a big sweep over the territory above the ranch, but they found no cougar tracks.

"Don't think of leaving yet," Mr. Morton said when the two returned to report. "You know you're more than welcome to stay with us until you do pick up the cat's trail. This snow will drive the deer and elk down to less snowy feeding grounds. If the cougar's in the higher country, he'll follow them down."

Snow continued to fall for three days, and the hunters didn't leave the ranch; but the sun was out on the fourth day, and no snow was in the air. "It's a little early in the season for eight inches of snow here at the ranch," Mr. Morton said. "It could be twice as deep up near the mountains."

"We'll get all set today for staying out several days, in case it's necessary," Mr. McClung decided. "We'll carry food for both ourselves and the dogs. If we don't find the cougar's tracks near here, we'll strike as far north as the upper end of McDonald Lake."

Starting at daylight the next day, Ray and his father explored the territory above the ranch again, and then started north. It was noon before they found the tracks they were looking for.

"These were made early last night," Mr. McClung decided. "It stopped snowing before we went to bed, and there's a little loose snow in these tracks."

The dogs, after the hours of traveling, were in no great hurry. Following the meandering trail of the cougar, they came upon the remains of a doe it had killed and partly eaten. From this point the dogs took off in a more excited manner and at a faster pace.

"He won't be far from here," Mr. McClung said, as he and Ray hurried along. "He'll lay up with a full stomach."

The hunter's prediction proved correct when, half an hour later, the dogs' excited baying told them that the cougar had been jumped. Ray and his father sped up to keep within hearing distance of the dogs.

"He'll be logy from his big feed last night. He won't run long," Mr. McClung said. "This is quicker and easier than I imagined it might be. He'll soon tree."

"Can I shoot him out of the tree, Dad?" Ray asked.

"Yes, he's all yours. I think you have that coming," his father told him.

But a short time later the baying of the dogs

ceased. "Must have lost the trail," Ray panted, as they followed the tracks left by the four dogs.

But the dogs hadn't lost the trail. The men came upon their bodies on the bloody snow a short time later. The story was plainly read. The big cougar had passed between two great boulders, which came together, and had sprung to the top of one of them. When the four eager dogs had rushed into the space between the rocks, no more than twelve feet long, the cougar had dropped down behind them. The dogs were trapped. They had no chance to dodge away as they would have done in the open.

Gazing down sadly at the torn and mangled bodies, Mr. McClung said, "Poor dogs. Old Spot has treed forty cougars, and the younger dogs learned their trade well by running with him. This cat doesn't seem to have the ingrained fear of dogs that most cougars have. He outsmarted them. He must have brains as well as size."

They set about cutting brush to heap over the dogs. It was all they could do for them. Tears came to Ray's eyes when he laid the bloody body

of Old Spot beside the other three before piling the brush over them. "I wanted to kill the cougar before this," he told his father. "Now I know we *must* kill him. Old Gurgling Spring was right— he's a devil. For what he did to our dogs, I hate him as bad as the old woman says he hates me."

In the foot of snow which the storm had left, the cougar had printed a plain trail down into a deep canyon. The sides became steeper as Ray and his father advanced. The cougar had found it easy to spring to a ledge twenty feet below, but the men were slowed up as they proceeded carefully. Sometimes they were forced to take a roundabout way to find a less steep trail down.

Knowing that they might be in the woods over- night, they each were carrying two blankets with their food. At an elevation of five or six thousand feet, the nights would be cold.

The two men stopped to size up the steep, rocky slope they were about to descend. "Do you think we'll ever get close to him, Dad?" Ray asked.

Mr. McClung hesitated before answering. He had told the Mortons, "We'll stay on the trail until we get him." Now, without the dogs, the cougar would be hard to come up with.

"I've been pondering on that," he told Ray. "We might think this over a bit before going on. The cougar has always retreated to this cut-up section when he was hunted. He's familiar with the territory. We have plenty of food for several days, with the biscuits and dried meat we brought along for the dogs added to our own supply, and we can shoot grouse or a deer if necessary. If we worry this big cat by staying on his trail, he won't have time to hunt, and we might wear him down, but that will take time. I won't blame you a bit if you would rather turn back."

Ray, as was his way, considered carefully before replying. He looked out across the wild, broken country, and up at the peaks of a mountain range that towered a mile above them. Dark, shifting clouds gave proof that a blizzard was whirling about the summits. He weighed his words well as he answered his father.

"This cougar will never be caught by dogs. He seems to have lost all fear of even a whole pack, and he knows how to get rid of them. Perhaps, if we stay on his trail, we might eventually catch sight of him. He may become careless. Even a few seconds would be enough, if he were within range. I think we should go on."

His father gave him a look of quiet satisfaction. He had trained this sturdy son well by taking him on hunts even before he was big enough to pack a rifle. Ray would have disappointed him had he wanted to turn back. "Guess we may as well be starting on, then," he said.

But a little way down the slope disaster befell them. Mr. McClung lost his precarious footing on a steep, slippery face of rock, and slid swiftly to the foot of the slope, striking his ankle on a jutting point. When Ray reached him he was sitting up in the snow, feeling the injured foot.

"Broken just above the ankle," he said to Ray. "And after thirty years in the woods without an accident," he added in exasperation.

Ray gave his father a sympathetic look. "Well, it's a good thing you taught me always to carry a piece of string in my pocket, Dad," he said. "I'll

get a couple of sticks for splints, and wrap this strong string around them real tight.''

He bound up his father's foot carefully. ''That's a good job, Son,'' said Mr. McClung.

''Now we'll have to get you back up to the top of this slope,'' Ray replied. ''Wish we had a rope, but since we haven't, I'll trim a small sapling for a ladder. You can crawl up while I hold the upper end.''

Ray sat at the top of the slope with the slender pole held firmly in his hands and his heels braced in a crevice in the ledge. His father slowly dragged himself to the top. The remainder of the climb was not so difficult, but an hour was consumed before they were out of the canyon.

"As soon as I get you fixed for the night, Dad, I'll start back to the ranch," Ray said.

In a clear spot well away from the canyon, he scraped the snow off the carpet of leaves. "I'm leaving you all the blankets," he told his father, as he spread two of them on the ground. When Mr. McClung was comfortable with the two remaining blankets over him, Ray started a fire. Then he began to cut a supply of firewood. The fire was burning brightly by the time Ray had stacked up a pile of wood, cut from dry, dead limbs of fallen trees.

"I'll put this short, crotched pole beside you, Dad," he said. "You can sit up and toss wood into the fire and push it into position with the pole."

"Thanks, Son," his father said. "A fire near my feet will help keep them warm. I may go to sleep, though, and let the fire die down. You might wrap some of those dead pine twigs around the end of another pole. With the dry needles on them, they make a quick blaze for starting some more dry limbs to burning."

When all this had been accomplished Ray looked at his watch. "Four o'clock," he said. "Figuring from the time it took us to get here, I'd have a six-hour walk back in daylight, but it'll be dark in two hours. The moon will be out, though, and I'll keep going. I'll follow our tracks all the way back. Are you comfortable, Dad?"

"I'm fine, Son," his father assured him. "Mighty lucky that you were with me."

Chapter 9   WITH A DOGSLED

The last hour of his trip took all the determination Ray could muster. Laboring through the loose snow since daylight had tired him to the point of exhaustion, but he kept doggedly on. The moon had dropped below the treetops, and he had trouble in staying with the tracks he and his father had made that morning. Finally, deciding that he could hold his direction because he felt a woodsman's familiarity with the terrain, he abandoned the trail. He felt an overwhelming relief when he came in sight of the darkened ranch house.

After listening to Ray's story, Mr. Morton said, "I'll go down and ask Charlie Hopp to come up with his dog team. It's the only way we can get your father out. And there's no use trying to go anywhere with the sled while it's dark. We'll start at daylight. You seem to have left him well taken care of."

Mrs. Morton had stirred up the fire. "Get your boots off, Ray," she ordered, "and have something to eat. I bet you're plenty hungry."

After disposing of a quantity of venison stew, and half a dozen doughnuts with his coffee, Ray was so nearly asleep that Mrs. Morton sent him to bed. "Have a good sleep. I'll fix breakfast in time to get you off early," she assured him.

He was asleep one minute after sliding into bed, and when the start was made in the morning, with the four husky dogs in front of the long sled, he felt as fresh as ever.

The dogs mushed steadily along, with Ray taking the lead to show the way. They found Mr. McClung sitting up in his blankets. The small bucket used for making tea was among the coals. "Had you figured to be along about now," he greeted them.

"Dad!" Ray cried, after taking one look at him. "What's happened? There's blood all over the front of your shirt, and it's running down your arm, too!"

His father's handkerchief was wrapped about his throat, and a cloth from the food sack was wound around his arm. "Sit down and have some tea and eat your lunch," Mr. McClung answered. "I'll tell you all about it." He would say no more till they were all seated around the remains of the fire. Then he told them his story.

"My leg pained me some," he began, "and I woke up several times. I built the fire up a little every time, but toward morning I went to sleep for a couple of hours. When I woke up I lay still for a minute, looking up at the stars. The fire had died down to just a bed of coals. Something seemed wrong. I rolled my eyes a little without moving. Lucky I did. By the dim starlight, I observed a movement off beyond the fire. My eyes

grew accustomed to the darkness and I made out the dim form of something big creeping slowly—very slowly—toward me. It could be only one thing. I moved fast. With one motion I thrust the bundle of pine twigs you'd made up for me, Ray, into the coals and snatched the blanket over my head. The cougar must have made his spring at the same time. I felt his weight settle on me. His teeth sank through the blankets and made these gashes across my throat. His claws must have scratched my arm."

Mr. McClung wiped the perspiration off his forehead. "Puts me in a cold sweat to think about it," he continued. "Then he suddenly sprang away. I threw back the blankets and snatched at my rifle beside me. The flames had flared up as the dry needles struck the coals, and that had frightened him. I saw him make a long leap to the butt of that downed tree over there. He stopped a moment with a snarl in his throat. His lips were drawn back from his long, white fangs. I threw the rifle across my lap in time to make one snap shot as he left the log and was out of sight in the darkness."

Mr. McClung drew a great sigh of relief. "The good Lord must have awakened me from a sound sleep. I had no trouble staying awake after that. I kept comfortable, though a little snow fell after daylight. I prayed that you'd get here before night."

The men finished eating in silence. Then Charlie Hopp swung the dog team around so the sled was alongside the injured man, and he and Mr. Morton lifted him into the low box set on the runners. Mr. McClung eased back onto the blankets they had brought along, with a little grimace of pain as the splints on his leg dragged against the frame of the sled.

While this was being done, Ray had followed the trail of the cougar a short distance. He came back to report, "You hit him, Dad. He went away dragging his left hind leg, and there was blood on the trail. Too bad you didn't have just a half second more—you'd have drilled him through the middle. He'll find traveling and hunting pretty tough now. Well, I'll make a pack of the rest of this stuff. The dogs will need help on the way back, with the load they have now."

When Charlie Hopp started the dogs mushing on the way back to the ranch, Ray motioned for Mr. Morton to come back. "I kept these two blankets and the food sack because I'll need them," he told the rancher. "I'm taking the cougar's trail. He's badly wounded, and he can't travel far on three legs. If I don't get him today, I'll surely come up with him tomorrow. This cougar has proved that he's not afraid of people.

He's terribly cunning, too. Probably waited all night for the fire to die down. Not many wild animals would have come near a camp while there was a fire that even glowed. He's too dangerous to be permitted to run loose any longer." There was a hard look in Ray's blue eyes as he finished. "He tried to kill my dad. No cat is going to get away with that."

"Your father will never consent to this, Ray," Mr. Morton protested.

"Don't tell him until you're well away," Ray answered. He was rolling the two blankets and the sack of food into a neat bundle as he spoke. "I'm leaving right now." He started to strap the pack onto his shoulders.

Realizing how useless it would be to protest, the rancher helped Ray fasten his pack, and told him, "All I can do is wish you luck, I guess. You may need it, boy." He gave Ray a slap on the back. "I can hardly call you a boy anymore," he concluded. "You're big and strong, and few of your age have had more experience in the woods."

Before starting to catch up with the sled, Mr. Morton watched Ray as he moved swiftly along on the trail of the killer. "Older than his years," he told himself with a shake of his head.

Chapter 10   RAY TAKES THE TRAIL

The trail led straightaway for a mile, then Ray came to a place where the cougar apparently had stopped to lick its wound. He judged that the animal had remained some time at this spot. There was a round, well-packed depression in the snow, colored with blood. The track leading away showed that the cougar had walked with short steps, and a furrow in the snow indicated it had been dragging its injured left leg. Ray assumed that the bullet had broken the bone somewhere below the hip.

Holding a fast pace, and keeping a keen watch ahead, Ray avoided passing near high outcroppings of rock from which his quarry might launch an attack. He was puzzled when the tracks led him in a circle back toward his father's campsite. This surprising beast had walked up the sloping trunk of a tree which had broken off about twenty feet above the ground, but which was still propped up on the tall stump. From this point of vantage it had doubtless watched the man and his fire. Ray remembered his father's remark that snow had fallen after daylight. There was no snow in the tracks leading away. This discovery meant the cougar had lingered till morning, watching and waiting. Ray now was more convinced than ever that he was dealing with a very vindictive and determined foe.

He maintained his speed throughout the day, and stopped well before dark to prepare for the night. His preparations consisted mainly in cutting a plentiful supply of wood, for he would sit in the center of three fires this night. There would

be no sleep for him, Ray resolved. He might be master of the situation during the daylight hours, but he would concede the advantage to his opponent during the hours of darkness.

At the first sign of daylight, Ray melted snow for the tea which made the dry provisions more satisfying. Remembering the cougar's actions of the previous day, he scouted the area all around his camp. Sure enough, the cougar had circled the camp twice before taking up a station where it could observe Ray sitting between his fires.

All day Ray followed the tracks at a steady pace. He was sure the cougar wasn't far ahead. He became doubly cautious. If the animal's tracks entered a thick growth of evergreens, Ray circled around to the point where the trail left the cover. Once his quarry must have remained in such a place till Ray started his circling, for the outgoing tracks showed the cougar had left the thicket at a run—the only time it had moved faster than a walk, which was easier on its wounded hip. Now, with the day about to end, Ray was faced with another sleepless night.

It was a night he would never forget. Keeping awake the previous night had not been easy, but this one became a night of horror. Tired from two days of travel, and sleepless for thirty-six hours, Ray found it increasingly difficult to stay awake as the night advanced. He brewed tea, sang songs, and recited all the poetry he could remember. He danced, did calisthenics—anything he could think of to keep his drooping eyelids from closing. He had no delusions as to what would be his fate should the flame of his fires die out while he sat on his blankets, fast asleep.

He could picture the cautious approach of the great cat, stealing soundlessly nearer and nearer as the fires died away. Then the swift spring, the moment of terror as the long fangs pierced his throat, then—nothing. Sometime some hunter might find his scattered bones and the charred remains of his fires.

Within the campsite Ray felt reasonably safe, but he never permitted himself to forget the menace somewhere beyond the lighted circle. His rifle he kept always at hand.

When bright daylight came, Ray again started out. Dead tired, he was nonetheless glad to be moving. He felt certain he would come up with the cougar before night. He knew it hadn't eaten during the past two days. With the added handicap of the useless leg, it would be desperately tired. He would exercise special caution, he determined.

His first narrow circle around his camp cut the tracks of the cougar coming in and also leaving the vicinity. It had observed the camp from a ridge of rock less than a hundred yards away. The outgoing tracks appeared to be very fresh.

One thing in his favor, Ray reflected, was that the cougar was making no attempt to use rough territory, as it had before it was hurt. It was sticking to the wooded hillsides and flats. Apparently it realized that climbing down and up the steep sides of rocky canyons was too strenuous to be attempted with its useless leg. It had reversed its line of travel, and was proceeding in the general direction of the ranch.

After resting at noon, when he ate a little food and fought sleep for half an hour, Ray pressed on. Surely, he considered, the animal ahead of him was as worn out as himself.

He was elated when he caught his first glimpse of the long, tawny form, as it came out of a clump of bushes and crossed over a ridge, tiredly dragging the injured leg. The distance was too great for a shot; the cougar was keeping just far enough ahead to be safe. With his spirits revived, Ray hurried along the trail. "Maybe," he mumbled to himself, "he'll stop to rest and I'll get close enough for a shot."

But this proved a vain hope. The tracks led on and on, with the animal never again showing itself. As the afternoon advanced, Ray became desperately sleepy. He caught himself stumbling. "I simply must get a few minutes of sleep," he told himself, "or the cougar will be sure to outlast me."

He began casting about in his mind for some method of accomplishing this. Soon he came to an overhanging, clifflike outcropping of rock, almost a cave. The cougar had passed around this high point. Ray followed the trail a hundred yards and turned back. He cut a slender sapling and a crotched stick. The stick he drove into the snow, placing some rocks around it to keep it erect. Laying the middle of the sapling in the crotch, he put a heavy rock on its small end. This tilted the heavy end several feet off the ground and well back under the cliff. Next he cut some long, dry limbs for firewood, which he laid out so their ends rested under the small tip of the sapling. Packing small twigs among the sticks of wood, he lit the end of the pile farthest from the pole. When the fire was well started, he threw himself down under the heavy end of the sapling. He was depending upon the fire to burn toward the sapling, catch the tree itself, and burn it through. That would release the rock on the small end, and the large end would fall onto Ray and awaken him. He estimated this would require at least thirty minutes; it was a chance he had to take. He was asleep in an instant.

The heavy end of the pole striking Ray's shoulders aroused him and the thought of danger snapped him wide awake, his rifle in his hands. A glance at his watch showed he had been asleep forty minutes.

Greatly refreshed, he took up his stalk. There were a scant three hours of daylight left. He found that the cougar had circled around the crest of a hill to a point where it could see the smoke rising from the fire. Then it had entered one patch of timber after another, as though searching for something. Ray circled around all these. He didn't propose to be trapped in some thick growth of brush. But time was running out. He would soon be forced to stop and prepare for the night, and he knew he couldn't go through another night without falling asleep.

The cougar had entered a large patch of timber which clothed both sides of a coulee. While Ray was circling the tract, the sun became obscured by clouds and the air filled with fine snow. The temperature was falling. Ray looked off toward a high peak to the west, the peak from which he had been taking his bearings. It was swathed in clouds which promised bad weather. Daylight would soon fade.

Ray arrived back at the point where the tracks had entered the coulee. No tracks led out. He brushed the snow off a rock and sat down, for he had a decision to make.

Ray took stock of the position in which he found himself. The cougar was in the timber and he was sure it didn't intend to leave. It was probably worn out and ready to bring the pursuit to an end. He thought of the long night he had spent fighting sleep. The chance he could keep awake once more through the coming hours of darkness was remote. Ray rose and thumbed back the hammer of his rifle. He would go through.

The light under the pines was dim, almost a twilight. Ray proceeded slowly, very carefully. He was sure his eyes had never been sharper, nor his hearing keener. He closely examined every tree, rock, and bush as he advanced, his finger firm on the trigger of his cocked rifle. A single thought filled his mind—he must see his foe first, for only one of the two would leave the timber.

He passed halfway through the pines, widely skirting high rocky outcroppings that jutted from the sides of the coulee. Then he started up the opposite slope. The trees were thicker here and the terrain rougher. Now the trail led between two rock formations some twenty feet apart. Ray paused. He should circle these rocky points. But he couldn't afford to spend many more minutes in this fast-darkening coulee. He carefully scanned the trees and the outline of the ledges of rock, then he advanced.

A slight scraping sound caused him to swing quickly around. Rising above the top edge of the nearest rock was the head of the big cougar. Its ears were flat to its head, its lips curled back from the half-opened jaws, and its eyes gleamed with satanic fury.

Ray's rifle instantly found his shoulder. He pressed the trigger as the beast rose for its spring. Again he flipped the lever and pulled the trigger. Then the cougar's heavy weight struck the muzzle of his rifle and the force of the catapulting body drove him to the ground. His head struck the base of a tree sharply, and then Ray remembered no more.

Half an hour later Ray opened his eyes. His fuzzy senses didn't tell him at once where he was. Snow was no longer sifting down through the pines, and a full moon was struggling to shed its light between the drifting clouds. Realization of his situation struck Ray suddenly. He turned up on his elbow and looked around. There it lay—a great, tawny shape, not five feet away, a picture of streamlined strength and savage beauty. Some-

how the boy could feel no animosity for his fallen foe. After all, it had only followed the dictates of its wild nature. But there would be one less scourge for the deer, and one less worry for mothers of wandering children.

He rose stiffly, shivering with the cold that had chilled him to the bone while he was unconscious. His first act was to build a great fire around which he danced until he was warm clear through. Then, by the leaping firelight, he examined the dead cougar with a hunter's curiosity. His first bullet had pierced the chest. The second, the powder burns proved, had struck low on the throat, and had severed the spine—a great bit of good fortune, because the cougar could have done him plenty of damage before the shot in the chest had taken final effect.

Ray wished he could measure the body of the cougar. Then he remembered that his carbine was thirty-eight inches long. So, stretching the body of the cougar out straight, he measured off three lengths of his carbine from the tip of the nose down the length of the body and tail. Four or five inches of tail extended beyond the three lengths of the rifle.

He wondered how it had attained its great size. "Oh, well," he concluded, "some people grow to be giants, too, and no one really knows why."

Ray set about skinning the cougar, being careful not to gash the hide and to skin the head out cleanly. Reports of this cougar's size had spread all over the province, and one collector of unusual trophies had made a standing offer of one hundred dollars for its skin. Ray would collect the bounty, too.

He had been anything but sleepy while he was doing the skinning. His enforced rest when he was stretched out unconscious on the ground, as well as his excitement, had kept him wide awake. But now that he had finished he felt exhausted. His eyes were refusing to stay open. He spread out the great skin, fur side up, wrapped himself in his blankets, and lay down upon it. "A little smelly," he said to himself, grinning as he lapped the edges up over his feet, "but it will keep the cold out."

He scarcely had time to think how the scream-
ing jays and scolding chickadees would probably
wake him when the sun rose over the treetops,
before he was dead asleep.

VERNE T. DAVIS was born in Michigan, and during his boyhood spent much time exploring the woods and studying nature. Hunting and fishing were also strong interests in his life. From this background has come the material for his books.

Mr. Davis has lived in California for the past thirty years. Before that he worked in Wyoming and Texas and other parts of the United States. He was a construction superintendent for twenty-five years and also taught school for two years. He is married and has a daughter.